TINTIN'S TRAVEL DIARIES

Publisher's note:

Tintin, the intrepid reporter, first made his appearance January 10, 1929, in a serial newspaper strip with an adventure in the Soviet Union. From there, it was on to the Belgian Congo and then to America. Together with his dog, Snowy; an old seaman, Captain Haddock; an eccentric professor, Cuthbert Calculus; look-alike detectives, Thomson and Thompson; and others, Tintin roamed the world from one adventure to the next.

Tintin's dog, Snowy, a small white fox terrier, converses with Tintin, saves his life many times, and acts as his confidant, despite his weakness for whiskey and a tendency toward greediness. Captain Haddock, in some ways Snowy's counterpart, is a reformed lover of whiskey, with a tendency toward colorful language and a desire to be a gentleman-farmer. Cuthbert Calculus, a hard-of-hearing, sentimental, absent-minded professor, goes from small-time inventor to nuclear physicist. The detectives, Thomson and Thompson, stereotyped characters down to their old-fashioned bowler hats and outdated expressions, are always chasing Tintin. Their attempts at dressing in the costume of the place they are in make them stand out all the more.

The Adventures of Tintin appeared in newspapers and books all over the world. Georges Remi (1907–1983), better known as Hergé, based Tintin's adventures on his own interest in and knowledge of places around the world. The stories were often irreverent, frequently political and satirical, and always exciting and humorous.

Tintin's Travel Diaries is a new series, inspired by Hergé's characters and based on notebooks Tintin may have kept as he traveled. Each book in this series takes the reader to a different country, exploring its geography, and the customs, the culture, and the heritage of the people living there. Hergé's original cartooning is used, juxtaposed with photographs showing the country as it is today, to give a feeling of fun as well as education.

If Hergé's cartoons seem somewhat out of place in today's society, think of the time in which they were drawn. The cartoons reflect the thinking of the day, and set next to modern photographs, we learn something about ourselves and society, as well as about the countries Tintin explores. We can see how attitudes have changed over the course of half a century.

Hergé, himself, would change his stories and drawings periodically to reflect the changes in society and the comments his work would receive. For example, when it was originally written in 1930, *Tintin in the Congo,* on which *Tintin's Travel Diaries: Africa* is based, was slanted toward Belgium as the fatherland. When Hergé prepared a color version in 1946, he did away with this slant. Were Hergé alive today, he would probably change many other stereotypes that appear in his work.

From the Congo, Tintin went on to America. This was in 1931. Al Capone was notorious, and the idea of cowboys and Indians, prohibition, the wild west, as well as factories, all held a place of fascination.

Cigars of the Pharaoh (1934) introduced Hergé's fans to the mysteries of India. A trip to China came with *The Blue Lotus* in 1936, the first story Hergé thoroughly researched. After that, everything was researched, including revisions of previous stories.

Tintin's Travel Diaries are fun to read, fun to look at, and provide educational, enjoyable trips around the world. Perhaps, like Tintin, you, too, will be inspired to seek out new adventures!

The publisher particularly wishes to thank Mrs. Christine Ockrent and television channel Antenne 2 for their kind permission to use the title *Travel Diaries*.

TINTIN'S TRAVEL DIARIES

A collection conceived and produced by Martine Noblet.

Les films du sable thank the following **Connaissance du monde** photographers for their participation in this work:

Jean-Claude Berrier, Christian Monty, Michel Drachoussoff, Maximilien Dauber.

The authors thank Mac-Leo Felix and Christiane Erard for their collaboration.

First edition for the United States and Canada published by Barron's Educational Series, Inc., 1994.

All inquiries should be addressed to:
Barron's Educational Series, Inc.
250 Wireless Boulevard
Hauppauge, New York 11788

Library of Congress Catalog Card No.:94-13764

International Standard Book No. 0-8120-6425-9 (hard cover)
International Standard Book No. 0-8120-1864-8 (paperback)

Library of Congress Cataloging-in-Publication Data
Bruycker, Daniel de.
    [Carnets de route de Tintin, l'Afrique noire. English]
    Tintin's travel diaries, Africa / text by Daniel De Bruycker and Maximilien
Dauber ; translation by Maureen Walker.
        p.   cm.
    "Collection conceived and produced by Martine Noblet."
    Includes bibliographical references and index.
    ISBN 0-8120-6425-9. — ISBN 0-8120-1864-8 (pbk.)
    1. Africa—Description and travel—Juvenile literature.
[1. Africa. 2. Cartoons and comics.] I. Dauber, Maximilien.
II. Noblet, Martine. III. Title.
DT3.B73 1994   94-13764
960—dc20   CIP

Printed in Hong Kong
4567   9927   987654321

AFRICA

Text by Daniel De Bruyker and Maximilien Dauber

Translation by Maureen Walker

BARRON'S

TINTIN IN THE CONGO! or TINTIN IN SUB-SAHARAN AFRICA! Like me, he was probably one of the last few lucky enough to discover Africa, and to be filled with wonder by it. Those were the days when you still used to cross the Sahara on a jeep, guided by a compass, when Pygmies with lances hunted elephants in the forbidden forest, and when, lulled by the song of the dugout paddlers, daring travelers went up rivers where hippopotamus and crocodile swam.

I loved that Africa, now gone, with a passion—the Africa of explorers who lived out their dreams, the Africa that Tintin shows us again today.

JEAN-CLAUDE BERRIER

What I like about sub-Saharan Africa, from the Blue Nile to the Congo River, is its diversity. Extremes of landscape, many different people and customs. I've traveled there a lot, just for the pleasure of it.

Listen to African storytellers and other narrators of fantastic legends. Whether they accompany themselves on the *inanga** or on the *balafon**, they will tell you that the most important thing in their country is nature, and that it is imposing—grasslands, forests, rivers, trees (and even the gods that hide in them), and the emptiness of the desert. Now, changes in nature, if left alone, are measured not in the centuries but in millennia.

Africa is not always subject to reason. Why, for instance, is the land so poor, this land that produces cocoa, copper, and diamonds? No economist's explanation will give you the right answer.

As I see it, we have to understand Africa in some other way. Present-day Africa, even if most of it has been explored, mapped, and exploited, is still the continent of unlimited vastness and mystery.

CHRISTIAN MONTY

*Harp and xylophone from the East and West of Africa respectively.

CONTENTS

The words in **boldface** refer to the glossary beginning on page 70.

WHAT ARE THE GREAT REGIONS OF AFRICA?

From east to west, for 3,125 miles (5,000 km), Africa is traversed by the Sahara desert. The Sahara is what separates North Africa from sub-Saharan Africa.

O f the five continents, Africa, the second largest in area and third largest in population, is the one best known for its broad expanses of wilderness and torrid climate. Sub-Saharan Africa is usually divided into four large regions.

West Africa, situated between the **Sahara** and the Gulf of Guinea, is humid, fertile, and heavily populated. A string of ports lie along the coast, and around them small states have developed—Sierra Leone, Liberia, and Ghana, for example. The other big cities are found along the Niger, the most important river in the region.

Around the equator, Central Africa is an area dominated by humid forests. The abundant rainfall feeds the waters of enormous rivers like the Congo, whose vast basin constitutes the heart of the region.

The surface of East Africa, which is usually drier, is composed of high plateaus, mountains, and volcanoes. Big lakes are the sources of rivers such as the **White Nile** and the **Blue Nile**, which flow toward Egypt and the Mediterranean. Southern Africa, located in the southern hemisphere, is a rather arid region made up of huge grasslands and one of the largest of the African deserts, the Kalahari. Only the extreme south, with a warm, mild climate, provides rich farming. There are several islands in the Indian Ocean, the largest one being Madagascar, that are also populated by Africans.

Top:
Mount Kilimanjaro
(Kenya-Tanzania)
Bottom left:
Tibesti Mountains
in Chad
Bottom right:
Ahaggar Mountains
in the Algerian Sahara

WHERE DID MAN FIRST APPEAR?

Current research places the "cradle of civilization" in the eastern part of Africa, between Tanzania and Ethiopia.
In this area paleontologists discovered the oldest human skeletal remains known so far.

In the Great Rift Valley, primates known as **australopithecines** slowly evolved into present-day human beings, passing through various stages over millions of years. First there was *Homo habilis*, then *Homo erectus*. When the climate became drier, forests receded and human beings had to learn to survive in the grasslands and to walk upright in order to keep an eye out for their enemies or for their prey. With their hands freed, they soon learned to handle and make tools. They began to live in better organized groups, and as a result of the use of speech, *Homo erectus* evolved into *Homo sapiens*, the species to which we belong.

By studying fragments of skeletons and tools found on the sites at Olduvai (Tanzania), Lake Turkana (Kenya), and in the Omo Valley (Ethiopia), paleontologists have been able to recreate the beginning of the history of man. Gradually, the human groups migrated toward Europe and Asia, and much later toward Oceania and the Americas. As a result of the work of researchers, it is now known that all humans, beyond their physical differences, their cultures, their languages, and their customs, descend from the same family of African origin, the family of our distant ancestress, Lucy, an australopithecine from Ethiopia, who died at the age of 20, over three million years ago.

Left: Lake Nakuru (Kenya)

A prehistoric (Australopithecine) skull

3 WHY DO MOST AFRICANS HAVE DARK SKIN?

Skin color depends on exposure to sunlight, and the pigmentation that protects the skin from burns caused by the rays of the sun.

According to anthropologists, the first people probably had dark skin. Deprived of daily exposure to sunlight, Europeans are believed to have experienced, with the passage of generations, a lightening of the skin. Conversely, Africans are thought to have become gradually darker.

The dark-skinned peoples of Africa generally have tightly curled hair and characteristic features, but there are many differences among Africans. For instance, the Pygmies, like many forest dwellers all over the world, are of small stature, while other peoples, like the Dinka of the Upper Nile, are very tall and slender, and the Watusi, cattle raisers who live in the east central Africa, are extremely tall.

Skin color may vary from deep black to light brown, or even brown tinged with yellow among the San, or Bushmen, or a coppery red among the Pygmies. The difference in pigmentation is due to the amount of **melanin**, a brown pigment responsible for the dark color of the skin and that varies from one group of Africans to another.

Facial features, stature, and hair texture are characteristics that do not provide a typical picture of the African, because, as with all people, the variations from one individual to another are so great.

Top: A Bokonjo native (Uganda)
Bottom: A young Turkana girl (Kenya)

WHERE DOES THE NAME "AFRICA" COME FROM?

4

The Romans, whose famous Numidian warriors were Africans of Berber origin, gave the continent its name. The Arabic "Ifriqiya," Africa in Latin, was the name of ancient Tunisia.

L ittle is known about Africa's past, although we know, from fossils and cave paintings found in northern Africa, that people lived in Africa hundreds of thousands of years ago.

Long ago, in times of peace, the ancient Egyptians traded with **Nubia** (or the Sudan) and the country of Punt, identified as present-day Somalia. In 46 B.C., Julius Caesar created the province of Africa Nova. Later, Muslim Arabs established contact with the Africans. Their caravans crossed the Sahara to bring back the gold of the powerful kings of Mali, in exchange for salt and copper, while their ships followed the eastern coastline as far as Zanzibar in search of ivory and spices.

In the west as in the east, some of the kingdoms with which they traded converted, willingly or otherwise, to Islam, while the kings of Ethiopia, taking refuge in their mountains, became Christian (around 300 A.D.). The other kingdoms, situated far from the coasts where the Arab navigators put into port, remained mysterious and inaccessible to Europeans. Among them was the great **Bantu** state, in the Zambesi region, whose immense fortified enclaves, called Zimbabwe, still tower in the country that has chosen that name in memory of its glorious past.

Left: Egyptian ruins
Right: Cave paintings
in Tanzania

WHO WERE THE FIRST EXPLORERS OF AFRICA?

The Egyptians and the Phoenician sailors crossed the Red Sea and were the first to trade along the coasts of Africa. It is believed that they even went around the entire continent, returning by way of the Pillars of Hercules, the present-day Strait of Gibraltar.

A long land and sea routes or by sailing up the Nile, the Egyptians reached the land of Cush (present-day Sudan) and the remote areas of Eritrea and Somalia. It was Pharaoh Nechao II, in 7 B.C., who first gave the order to sail around Africa. The Phoenicians, who were skilled sailors, established colonies on the Atlantic seaboard. The Romans made incursions into the Sahara, which was still verdant at the time, especially to capture animals intended for the circus.

The Arabs later established trading posts on the west and east coasts of Africa, as well as inland, for the pursuit of the salve trade. They monopolized trade, and it was not until the fifteenth century that the first Portuguese sailors landed on the coasts of western Africa. It was only around 1800 that Europeans plunged into the continent that to them was still full of mystery. The nineteenth century was the century of famous explorers like Mungo Park, René Callié, **Teleki**, David Livingstone, Henry Stanley, Sir Richard Burton, and many other intrepid travelers.

Top and bottom left: An engraving of the explorer Teleki

Bottom right: A sailing expedition

WHO WERE THE SLAVERS?

The word "slaver" formerly referred to traders in African slaves and to the ships that took these slaves far away from their native lands.

The kidnapping of Africans and forcing them to become slaves goes far back in time, even though, until the Middle Ages, the Slavs (hence the name "slaves") were also victims of the traders. The Arabs resumed this trade, transporting the slaves through the Sahara or by sea routes.

It was for the agricultural development of North America that Europe gave the "Slave Trade" a practically industrial dimension. The number of men and women deported from the "Slave Coasts" of Africa is estimated at over 10 million.

The Portuguese, the French, and the British, with the help of local kings who sold their prisoners or their own subjects, engaged in this shameful and cruel trade until the mid-nineteenth century.

The African Slave Trade gradually came to an end, after being condemned by the Congress of Vienna in 1815 and outlawed by the Congress of the United States in 1807. Unfortunately, some families or tribes in Africa continue the tradition of slavery.

Capturing slaves (engraving)

WHAT CAN BE SAID ABOUT COLONIZATION?

From the nineteenth century to the 1960s, Europe exploited Africa by creating colonies there. Though efforts were made to modernize the African continent and bring European civilization to it, colonization was nevertheless advantageous to the Europeans.

In the eighteenth century, while the colonies in America broke away from Europe and became independent, explorers were dazzling the Europeans with the wealth of the African continent. The European countries then decided to exploit this "new world." To attempt to justify a sometimes brutal conquest, Africans were described as savages, living more or less in the Stone Age and practicing cannibalism, to whom the Europeans would bring Christianity, civilization, trade, and industry.

Around 1914, the conquest was complete and the whole of Africa, except for Ethiopia and Liberia, was under European subjection. The European countries divided the continent into vast areas to be exploited, regardless of the existing states or the way the peoples and tribes were distributed. France seized nearly all of western Africa, a good portion of the equatorial region, and the island of Madagascar. Britain occupied eastern and southern Africa. Germany, Portugal, and Spain had their share, too, and Belgium acquired the Congo, a territory 80 times its own size. Missionaries flooded into Africa by the thousands, opening schools and hospitals and converting the population to Christianity. The colonists exploited the mineral resources and built huge plantations. Engineers and technicians constructed highways, railroads, and cities, while colonial administrators tried to govern in the name of their parent state.

Left: Building a railroad in Mali
Right: Growing rice

WHAT IS THE FUTURE OF AFRICA?

The situation today in sub-Saharan Africa is critical. Famines, wars, dictatorships, ecological disasters, a catastrophic economy, and overpopulation are the major problems of this part of the continent.

Though the present situation in most of the countries of Africa is the result in part of colonial fallout, it also is partly the fault of the African leaders themselves. Obtaining their independence between 1945 and 1966, most African countries had to remain within colonial frontiers. Thus, many peoples found themselves artificially divided, or dominated by other, more powerful groups who rule through dictatorship.

Many countries are affected by problems related to underdevelopment. For instance, leaders supported by costly armies remain in power, and government services are overloaded and frequently inefficient. Even after decolonization, Africa is still held hostage by the industrialized countries, which are still buying its raw materials at low prices, fixing the price of agricultural products such as cocoa, coffee, and peanuts, and at the same time selling it machinery and industrial products at top price. The indebtedness resulting from this unfair trade plunges these countries into a state of chronic poverty, that plague of underdevelopment of which the Third World as a whole is the victim.

Unless the African people manage to control their demographic explosion and unless African farmers are taught to become self-sufficient and to produce food for their people, there is a danger of the African being engulfed in widespread famine like that suffered in Ethiopia and Somalia.

Top: Native dancers in Rwanda. Bottom: Abidjan at sunset

DO PEOPLE LIVE LONG IN AFRICA?

The African continent now has medical centers and hospitals, but tropical diseases, infant mortality, chronic undernourishment, and now AIDS place it among those areas of the planet where life expectation is the shortest.

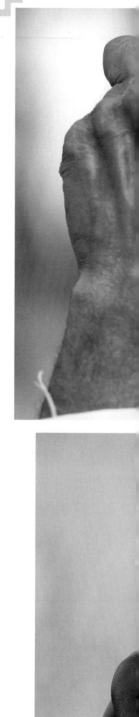

frica is afflicted by some diseases that are not encountered elsewhere, such as sleeping sickness, caused by the terrible tse-tse fly. Other so-called "tropical" diseases, such as leprosy or **malaria**, were formerly known, more or less, all over the world. Malaria was conquered by draining the marshes where mosquitoes—the anopheles that transmit the disease—used to teem. Today it is possible to purify water containing the worms and microbes that cause bilharzia (a parasitic infection that affects the bladder), dysentery, yellow fever, and others. But Africa, unfortunately, has not yet been able to complete the huge construction of public works required for improved sanitation, for drainage, and for treatment of drinking water, and therefore still falls victim to these illnesses. In addition, now there is the disturbing development of **AIDS**, which is thought to have begun on the African continent.

In addition to diseases affecting humans, cattle diseases, clouds of locusts, and droughts destroy the harvests and aggravate the problems of undernourishment. Despite all these plagues, the population, today only slightly better cared for and fed than in the past, is increasing very quickly, creating new problems. Since the harvests are insufficient to feed the rural inhabitants, millions of Africans flock to towns that are ill prepared to take them in. For lack of industries that would provide jobs and decent housing, many of them end up in the filth of the unsanitary shanty towns that are sprouting up in many places.

Top: A Lamu Muslim in Kenya
Bottom: A Samburu in Kenya

WHAT IS A TRIBE?

A tribe is a group of people who consider themselves descendants of the same ancestor. They usually accept the authority of one chief.

Hunting, farming, or raising cattle together, members of a tribe form a very well-knit group. They speak the same language and have the same religion and identical customs. They all obey the same chief or council of elders, in which the older members of each family participate. Men and women have different activities and meet in brother- or sisterhoods whose rites are kept secret. For instance, young men are admitted into the society of warriors after undergoing initiation. This initiation may consist of lengthy isolation in a sacred forest, a first lion hunt, circumcision, having their incisor teeth filed, or **scarification**.

Sometimes, to defend themselves from their neighbors, several tribes unite. The great kingdoms and empires of ancient Africa, such as the kingdoms of Benin, Gao, or Ghana, are believed to have arisen from this type of alliance.

Some of these peoples and tribes managed to survive during the colonial period. Some of them are now demonstrating their survival in the young independent states by banding together in "ethnically" based political parties. This phenomenon is disquieting in its effect on unity in these countries, and many African governments are trying to establish parties with a national vocation that will bring together people belonging to formerly rival tribes.

Left: Masai women
Right: Hairstyling among Masai men

WHAT LANGUAGES DO AFRICANS SPEAK?

With each group of people speaking its own language, the languages taught by the European colonists that are still learned in schools today often serve as the national language. For this reason, there is considerable risk that the most ancient cultures and local traditions will eventually disappear.

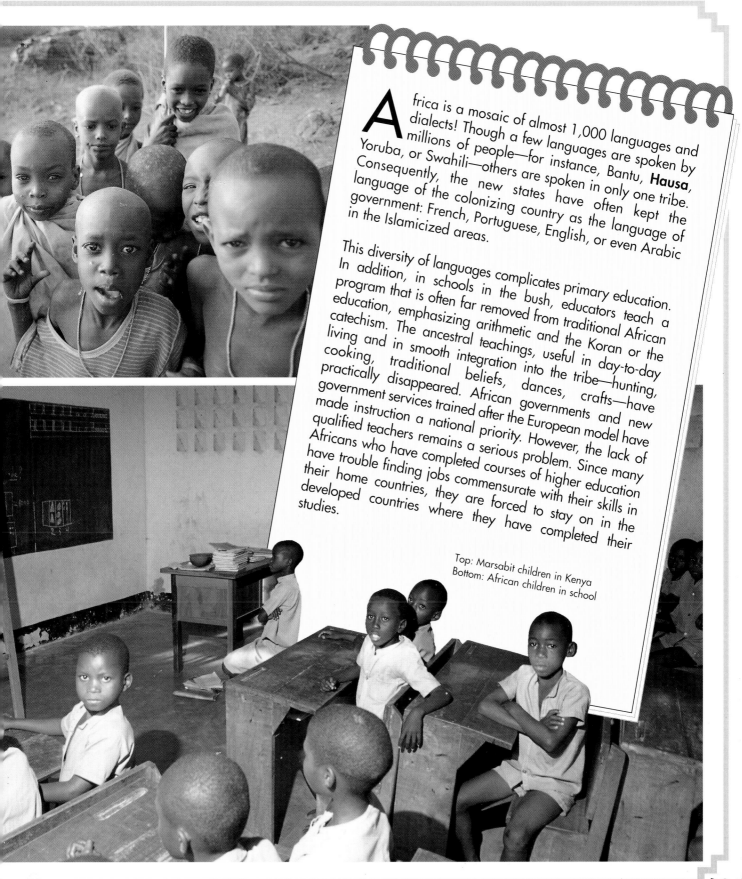

Africa is a mosaic of almost 1,000 languages and dialects! Though a few languages are spoken by millions of people—for instance, Bantu, **Hausa**, Yoruba, or Swahili—others are spoken in only one tribe. Consequently, the new states have often kept the language of the colonizing country as the language of government: French, Portuguese, English, or even Arabic in the Islamicized areas.

This diversity of languages complicates primary education. In addition, in schools in the bush, educators teach a program that is often far removed from traditional African education, emphasizing arithmetic and the Koran or the catechism. The ancestral teachings, useful in day-to-day living and in smooth integration into the tribe—hunting, cooking, traditional beliefs, dances, crafts—have practically disappeared. African governments and new government services trained after the European model have made instruction a national priority. However, the lack of qualified teachers remains a serious problem. Since many Africans who have completed courses of higher education have trouble finding jobs commensurate with their skills in their home countries, they are forced to stay on in the developed countries where they have completed their studies.

Top: Marsabit children in Kenya
Bottom: African children in school

WHAT RELIGIONS DO AFRICANS PRACTICE?

In addition to Islam and Christianity, which are widespread in Africa, many Africans still follow the traditional beliefs of their own tribes, based on communication with their ancestors.

Hunting tribes honor the powers of the land, nomadic shepherds those of the sun and the rain, and farmers practice the cult of their ancestors, convinced that the souls of the dead continue to reside among the living. Through rites and ceremonies, all of them commune with the spirits of nature (animism) to ensure good hunting, fertility, and protection for members of the tribe.

Many Africans believe in the power of magic. Healers practice exorcism to chase evil spirits out of the bodies of the sick, and prescribe medications made from flowers, leaves, tree bark, or roots. Fetishists consult the ancestors in the form of statues sculpted in their memory. Soothsayers establish the days for marriages or hunting, and magicians and rainmakers predict the weather for harvest days or festivals.

Some priests, who practice animal sacrifices in order to get into the good graces of a particular divinity, enjoy great respect. All these beliefs, though they are challenged by Islam or Christianity, are still very much alive in many regions of Africa, and are usually practiced alongside one or another of the imported **monotheistic** religions.

Top: A mosque in Mali
Bottom: Dogon masks

WHAT IS A "GRIOT"?

Poet, storyteller, and musician, the "griot" or African chronicler is the living memory of his people. He passes on from generation to generation all the wealth of his tribe's tradition.

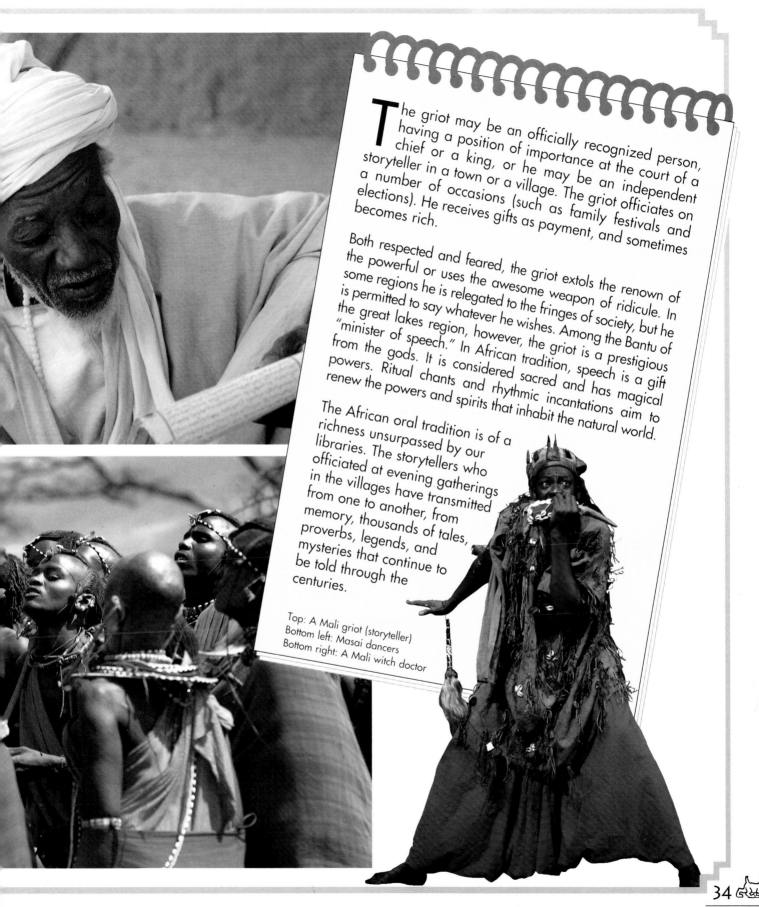

The griot may be an officially recognized person, having a position of importance at the court of a chief or a king, or he may be an independent storyteller in a town or a village. The griot officiates on a number of occasions (such as family festivals and elections). He receives gifts as payment, and sometimes becomes rich.

Both respected and feared, the griot extols the renown of the powerful or uses the awesome weapon of ridicule. In some regions he is relegated to the fringes of society, but he is permitted to say whatever he wishes. Among the Bantu of the great lakes region, however, the griot is a prestigious "minister of speech." In African tradition, speech is a gift from the gods. It is considered sacred and has magical powers. Ritual chants and rhythmic incantations aim to renew the powers and spirits that inhabit the natural world.

The African oral tradition is of a richness unsurpassed by our libraries. The storytellers who officiated at evening gatherings in the villages have transmitted from one to another, from memory, thousands of tales, proverbs, legends, and mysteries that continue to be told through the centuries.

Top: A Mali griot (storyteller)
Bottom left: Masai dancers
Bottom right: A Mali witch doctor

IS THE TOM-TOM A MUSICAL INSTRUMENT?

The tom-tom is a wooden drum made from a hollowed-out tree trunk or thick branch. It is more than a simple musical instrument; it also acts as the "African telegraph."

BOM
BOM
BOM

Just as church bells in the past were rung as warning signals, or as trumpets were blown on battlefields, the tom-tom is the "voice of the tribe," transmitting messages, exciting men in times of war, and accompanying happy occasions. Africa has thousands of tom-toms of all shapes and sizes, often grouped into large bands. African music associates complicated rhythms with chants that have many refrains and with dances that bring the entire population together. The tom-tom plays a key role in traditional life. No religious, civil, or family occasion could take place without this great music.

Rhythms, chants, and dances were brought to America by slaves, and were adapted to modern instruments. Today, they are enjoyed all over the world, and have names such as jazz, rock, samba, salsa. . . . African musicians also play the harp and the xylophone, which is the instrument the griot uses to accompany himself. The sanza, or "thumb piano," a small wooden box on which thin metal plates vibrate, is played to while away the time on long marches or to let villagers know someone is approaching.

Rwandan tom-toms (drums)

WHAT IS MEANT BY AFRICAN ART?

African art stunned a whole generation of European artists, who did not always realize to what extent the art was inseparable from tribal and religious life.

W hether sculptor, dancer, or singer, African artists always work primarily for a ritual purpose. Their religious beliefs are the main source of inspiration for their art. Statues of ancestors portray the serenity of the deceased in the afterlife, and a restrained strength of God the creator. They are primarily sacred objects and are made of wood, bronze, ivory, or clay. A son will respect the statue representing his deceased father, and address his prayers to it. Some statues contain **gris-gris**, such as crushed buffalo horn or crushed dried plants. African masks often portray spirits and are used to exorcise magical powers.

Though African artists find inspiration in the world around them, they do not copy it and do not try to be realistic. They interpret what they see and idealize it, leading to the impression of harmony emanating from the work. Painters like Picasso, Modigliani, Vlaminck, the Fauvists, and the Cubists used African art as inspiration for finding new ways of portraying the human figure and escaping from the conventions of academic painting.

Left: An African Luba mask
(Zaire)
Right: An African Kuba
mask (Zaire)

38

HOW DO AFRICANS ADORN THEMSELVES?

Jewels, headdresses, certain hairstyles, tattoos, and scarification belong to a whole tradition characteristic of traditional Africa—that of embellishing the body.

In the African tradition, the body is considered to be the bearer of a vital force residing mainly in the head, the sexual organ, the heart, and the blood. To protect these parts from evil spirits, some people use ritual signs. In some regions, the teeth are filed and the ears and the wings or the septum of the nose are pierced and adorned with jewels. The lips of Saras women in Chad, for instance, are sometimes distended by insertion of a wooden disk, called a "labret." Tattooing and scarification are usually practiced when an adolescent officially becomes an adult.

Jewels and headdresses, belts made of beads, or necklaces of leopard teeth also play a magical role in protection. Hairstyles may be very elaborate; the hair may be braided, and decorated with pendants. It is often the men who wear the most elaborate costumes.

In the past, African clothing consisted mostly of the headdress, leaving the body naked except for a loincloth. Under the influences of Christianity and Islam, suits have been adopted, but also popular are robes in dazzling colors and flowing **djellabas** in western Africa. Many men wear turbans, and women often wear veils. People usually go barefoot or wear sandals outside of the cities.

Left: A Rwandan dancer
Right: A Masai girl

WHAT WOULD ONE FIND ALONG THE NIGER RIVER?

When one travels the 2,615 miles (4,184 km) of the Niger River, one sees all the aspects of life in western Africa, from the mountains of Guinea to the marshes of Nigeria, by way of Tombouctou (Timbuktu) at the gateway to the desert.

Following the banks of the Niger River from its sources to its delta, one meets people whose lifestyles have changed little over the centuries, like the Dogon in Mali, who are farmers and artists. Lower down the river live the Songhai, formerly masters of the trade trails linking sub-Saharan Africa to the Maghreb. In the fifteenth and sixteenth centuries, the ambassadors of the Songhai emperors astonished the courts of Europe by presenting sumptuous gifts such as giraffes, animals not known in Europe that caused quite a stir. Their capital, Tombouctou (Timbuktu), was famous for its mosques that were made of unbaked clay. Until the eighteenth century, Timbuktu was a large marketplace for salt and slaves.

The **Yoruba** built large cities in the southwest of present-day Nigeria. The Ooni, their religious chief, had his headquarters at Ife, the holy city. The Yoruba were excellent craftsmen, sculpting impressive masks and statues in honor of their gods. They are still honored today, in the voodoo cult that the descendants of slaves have perpetuated in Latin America and in the Caribbean countries. The Ibo are farmers, occupying the plateaus in Lower Niger. They grow yams in the forest or work in the palm groves. There are many Ibo and they are highly protective of their autonomy, playing an important part in the political and economic life of Nigeria.

Left: The Niger River

Right: A Dogon mask

WHAT IS THE SAHEL?

The Sahara is a desert composed of sand and stone. On the edge of the Sahara is the Sahel, a huge area that is still slightly wooded, in the process of desertification.

Every year it becomes more difficult for farmers to survive in this area.

Around 6,000 years ago, the Sahara was a fertile land with fish-bearing rivers flowing through hills where game used to hide. The rock paintings and drawings left by Africans on the walls of the **Tassili**-n-Ajjer region of Algiers prove this. They depict men tending their sheep, hunting giraffe, or dancing. This entire civilization disappeared after climatic changes, and the Sahara became a vast expanse of desert where only the nomadic Tuaregs survive, moving from well to well on their camels.

One has to go much farther south to find game-stocked grasslands and the first farmers who stayed in one place, battling sand and drought to protect their meager harvests. The desert spreads a little farther every year and the inhabitants of the Sahel are often forced to relocate in the shantytowns around big cities. Yet it does rain sometimes in these regions, and drought is not the only cause of desertification. By constantly cutting down trees for firewood, people leave the soil too exposed to the sun and the winds, which destroy the thin layer of arable land. As wood becomes scarce, animal manure is used as fuel, to the detriment of the meager crops that are much in need of the precious fertilizer, the only one available.

Left: Salt plains in Dankali
(Denakil), Ethiopia
Right: The remains of camels
in the Chalbi Desert,
Kenya

WHAT SORT OF FOOD DO AFRICANS EAT?

African agriculture is devoted primarily to crops intended for export. Therefore, too little space and too few hands are left to develop the food crops that would feed the entire population.

Cereals such as barley, millet, and sorghum are the staple foods in the dry regions, while yams, sweet potatoes, and cassava are grown in the humid regions. Vegetables, such as peas and beans, are grown, as well as plantains (banana-like fruit) and pineapples, and oil-producing plants such as palm. In western Africa corn and rice provide some of the staples. Meat, once provided by hunting, is often replaced by fresh or dried fish, goat's meat, and poultry. Some people, such as the Pygmies, have continued to be hunters. They pound the meat of antelope and hippopotamus, wrap it in leaves, and cook it in ashes.

Not all Africans are fortunate enough to live in a region where there is game. The climatic conditions and the chronic disorganization in agricultural production result in shortages, constantly leading to famine among the ever-growing population. The strong influence of a tradition that does not believe in birth control and that leaves the hardest work to women rather than using animals for farming labor does nothing to improve matters. If we are to prevent the endemic famine that is going to spread across this continent where millions of people are already suffering from malnourishment, modernization of agriculture and radical changes in attitudes are essential.

Top: A market on the Ivory Coast
Bottom left: Grains in the Bamako market in Mali
Bottom right: A young woman carrying fruit

46

WHICH IS THE MOST POWERFUL RIVER IN AFRICA?

The Congo River, 12.5 miles (20 km) wide in some places, is the most powerful river in Africa. It drains the abundant water from an immense and perpetually wet basin, covered by the great equatorial forest.

Though the Nile, with its approximately 4,145 miles (6,671 km), is the world's longest river, the Congo is a veritable "ocean river," swollen by huge tributaries such as the Ubangi, the Uele, or the Kasai. Its nearly 3,000-mile (4,700 km) course is interspersed with rapids and flows through the Crystal Mountains, crossing the impressive Livingstone Falls before rushing into the Atlantic. The show is continuous along the river: hippopotamus and crocodile bathe in it, while herds of elephants wander along its banks or bathe in it. Under a torrid sun, natives fish for catfish.

In the dark forest, sparsely populated and difficult to reach, where the precious ebony wood abounds, the climate is unhealthy because of the marshes. This forest extends over five countries: Zaire, Congo, Gabon, Cameroon, the Central African Republic, and Equatorial Guinea. The Pygmies remain best able to cope with the difficult living conditions in the equatorial forest. Small in stature, with coppery red skin, they live by gathering and hunting. They are excellent musicians and dancers, and have preserved an impressive heritage of legends about the origin of the world and their god, whose hunting bow is the rainbow.

Top: A hippopotamus
Bottom left: Two elephants
Bottom right: A scene on the Niger River

21

WHAT IS "ADOBE ARCHITECTURE"?

Though African cities are accumulating concrete cubes, as are all major cities throughout the world, a large number of villages built of unbaked clay are still tucked away in the countryside. Their architecture and the materials used are as attractive as they are ingenious.

In Africa, adobe architecture is incredibly varied. Perfectly suited to the climatic conditions, it usually uses blocks of clay as the basic material. When the building reaches a given height, it is strengthened with a wooden framework, as are the minarets of mosques in Mali or in Niger. The thickness of the walls, the play of light and shadow, the openings, and the skillfully planned spaces make these adobe structures cool oases of refined beauty.

Climatic variations and differences in traditions lead to great variety in African dwellings. There are large, long huts, their roofs covered with a latticework of wooden sticks and big leaves cut into strips, all waterproofed with a coating of clay. Others are smaller and crowded together, like those of the Dogon, while still others are tall and come to a point, like the shell-shaped huts in North Cameroon. In Kenya, the Masai cover their houses with manure, while the Turkana use cattle hides. The Pygmies, who move frequently, make do with more rudimentary shelters made of wood and leaves. Whatever the style of the dwelling, the overall design, and the distribution of living space among the members of the tribe, these details always conform to a very strict symbolic code.

Adobe buildings

22

WHERE ARE THE SOURCES OF THE NILE?

The Nile rises in one of the most irregular landscapes on the planet. A region where, as they collided, two plates of the earth's crust forced up high mountains and volcanoes, which hollowed out the great ditch of the Rift, creating immense lakes in the process.

The Rift fault zone extends from the Jordan Valley to the Indian Ocean, passing through Ethiopia, Kenya, Tanzania, and Mozambique. The high Ruwenzori mountain range, in the west, has been known since ancient times as the Mountains of the Moon. The snow-capped summits, reaching a height of nearly 17,000 feet (5,118 m) feed into, when the snow melts, one of the sources of the Nile. East Africa consists mainly of fertile plateaus and hills where farmers and sheepherders have been settled for 2,000 years. They have terraced the steep slopes where, since colonial times, they have been growing plantains, coffee, and tea.

These farmers usually live in harmony with the traditionally more warlike herdsmen who watch over their large herds with pride. Seven big lakes formed in the bottom of the Rift, of which the largest, Lake Victoria, is a paradise for birds, in particular the heron, the ibis, and the pink flamingo. Tribes of fishermen live on the banks. Two volcanoes with snow-covered peaks look down upon the plain. They are Kilimanjaro—19,340 feet (5,895 m) high and Mount Kenya—17,058 feet (5,199 m) high.

The Mountains of the Moon in Ruwenzori, Uganda

23

WHO ARE THE MASAI?

The Masai are one of the best-known tribes of herdsmen. Their herds of longhorn cattle graze on the grasslands of eastern Africa.

The Masai live on the highlands of Kenya and North Tanzania, where they have finally settled permanently. They travel with their herds of cattle, sheep, and goats, avoiding the tse-tse fly-infested valleys. In the dry season, they look for water holes and grazing land. Their entire lives are organized around the herd, and they are as much its servants as its masters. They are very proud of their cattle, and are inclined to look down on their farmer cousins. Although they are herdsmen, they do not eat much meat. They feed themselves on the cows' milk and on their blood, taken directly from the jugular vein with a deft and painless arrow cut.

At the age of 15, a young Masai boy becomes a Moran. Released from caring for the herd, he then lives as part of a group of adolescents, learning the customs of adults and how to handle weapons. In the past, before the authorities prohibited it, there used to be a big hunt during which he had to kill a lion, and after that the Masai became a warrior at last. Later, he becomes head of a family with his own herd. In later life, he retires and devotes himself to religious duties. These "age classifications" set the pace of life all over Africa. Having come from the **Nilotic** regions, the Masai are related to the Dinka or Shilluk shepherds of southern Sudan and to the Samburu who live in northern Kenya. There are some startling resemblances between these proud herdsmen in East Africa and the nomadic Peuhl of West Africa, which suggests that the once-green Sahara made great migrations possible.

Top: Young Masai
      woman and baby
      (Kenya)
Bottom left:
Masai warriors
Bottom right:
A Masai taking
blood from a cow

24

WHERE WERE KING SOLOMON'S MINES LOCATED?

The love affair between King Solomon and the Queen of Sheba resulted in the birth of the first king of the "Lions of Judah" dynasty, who reigned over Ethiopia and its legendary gold mines.

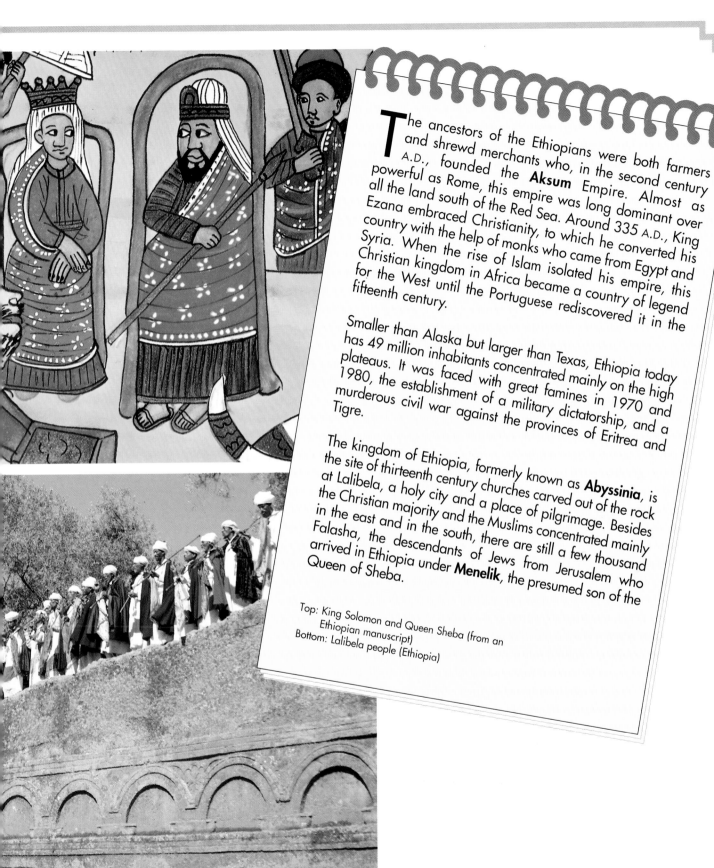

The ancestors of the Ethiopians were both farmers and shrewd merchants who, in the second century A.D., founded the **Aksum** Empire. Almost as powerful as Rome, this empire was long dominant over all the land south of the Red Sea. Around 335 A.D., King Ezana embraced Christianity, to which he converted his country with the help of monks who came from Egypt and Syria. When the rise of Islam isolated his empire, this Christian kingdom in Africa became a country of legend for the West until the Portuguese rediscovered it in the fifteenth century.

Smaller than Alaska but larger than Texas, Ethiopia today has 49 million inhabitants concentrated mainly on the high plateaus. It was faced with great famines in 1970 and 1980, the establishment of a military dictatorship, and a murderous civil war against the provinces of Eritrea and Tigre.

The kingdom of Ethiopia, formerly known as **Abyssinia**, is the site of thirteenth century churches carved out of the rock at Lalibela, a holy city and a place of pilgrimage. Besides the Christian majority and the Muslims concentrated mainly in the east and in the south, there are still a few thousand Falasha, the descendants of Jews from Jerusalem who arrived in Ethiopia under **Menelik**, the presumed son of the Queen of Sheba.

Top: King Solomon and Queen Sheba (from an Ethiopian manuscript)
Bottom: Lalibela people (Ethiopia)

WHAT IS A SAFARI?

The word "safari" means "journey" in Swahili. It used to be a hunting expedition of the sort that had always been practiced by warriors. In colonial times, Europeans soon developed a taste for it.

The time of the great safaris organized by white hunters through the bush has ended. The African states, fearing the disappearance of the species that constitute the beauty and wealth of the African fauna, have created vast wildlife parks where the animals are protected from hunters. In these numerous national parks, lions, leopards, elephants, giraffes, cheetahs, and hippopotamuses all live together, making Africa a paradise for nature lovers and camera enthusiasts. Thus emerged the photo-safari that enables us to admire gazelles, lions, and other wild animals in their natural habitat.

Though the wild animals that inhabit Africa are still very numerous and of great variety, the balance is nevertheless fragile. In Kenya, despite the prohibition of hunting, the Masai have continued to kill lions during their ritual hunts, and poachers have taken over from the hunters. Despite many campaigns, Africans are not always aware of the irremediable losses threatening their heritage, which makes up a sizeable amount of their tourism-related income.

Top: A lion hiding in the grass
Bottom: A kudu (a type of antelope)

26

WHY IS THERE ILLEGAL TRADE IN IVORY?

In addition to gold, ivory has always been the most coveted African resource.

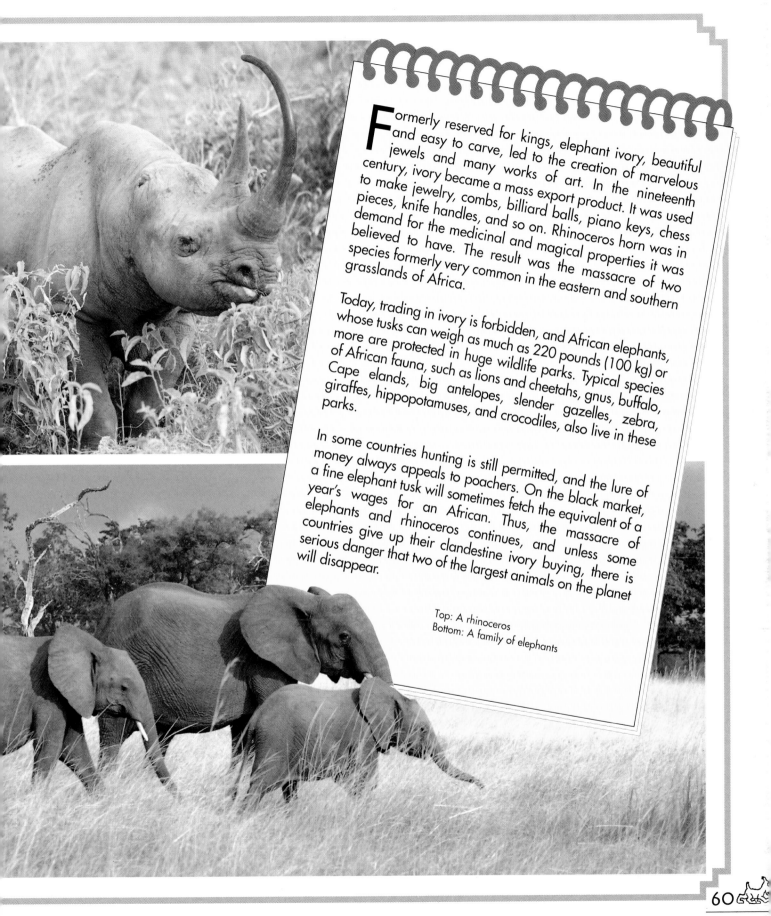

Formerly reserved for kings, elephant ivory, beautiful and easy to carve, led to the creation of marvelous jewels and many works of art. In the nineteenth century, ivory became a mass export product. It was used to make jewelry, combs, billiard balls, piano keys, chess pieces, knife handles, and so on. Rhinoceros horn was in demand for the medicinal and magical properties it was believed to have. The result was the massacre of two species formerly very common in the eastern and southern grasslands of Africa.

Today, trading in ivory is forbidden, and African elephants, whose tusks can weigh as much as 220 pounds (100 kg) or more are protected in huge wildlife parks. Typical species of African fauna, such as lions and cheetahs, gnus, buffalo, Cape elands, big antelopes, slender gazelles, zebra, giraffes, hippopotamuses, and crocodiles, also live in these parks.

In some countries hunting is still permitted, and the lure of money always appeals to poachers. On the black market, a fine elephant tusk will sometimes fetch the equivalent of a year's wages for an African. Thus, the massacre of elephants and rhinoceros continues, and unless some countries give up their clandestine ivory buying, there is serious danger that two of the largest animals on the planet will disappear.

Top: A rhinoceros
Bottom: A family of elephants

27

WHAT IS "APARTHEID"?

In Afrikaans, the language of the Boers, the word "apartheid" means "separation." It is a policy of racial segregation.

Conquered in the eighteenth century by Netherlands emigrants, the **Boers,** South Africa today is the richest and most highly industrialized country on the African continent. After most of the colonized countries had achieved independence, southern Africa remained in the hands of a minority of white colonists, refusing to recognize equal rights for the black population, and installing apartheid as the political system.

The minority whites own the gold and diamond mines, the rich farmlands, and all the Cape region with its vineyards and its orchards. The others—blacks, people of mix race, and Indians—the majority, live on land that is arid and without mineral resources. These populations are therefore forced to look for work in areas dominated by whites. Denied voting rights, they have not been able to live in those areas nor to frequent establishments reserved for whites. The protests of the African National Congress and black leaders such as Bishop Desmond Tutu and Nelson Mandela, who was jailed for 27 years, and the growing indignation of the whole world, finally resulted in the abolition of this unjust system and steps toward the installation of power sharing among the various communities. In the spring of 1994 the first multiracial elections in South Africa were held, and Nelson Mandela was elected President.

A group of children in Kenya
Right: South Africa's Nelson Mandela

28

WHERE WAS THE WORLD'S BIGGEST DIAMOND FOUND?

The Cullinan diamond, the world's largest, was discovered in South Africa in 1905. It was presented to the king of England, and weighed 3,106 carats, or a little over 1 lb. 6 oz. (621 grams).

The diamond is far from being South Africa's sole treasure. The subsoil also contains gold, silver, platinum, uranium, chromium, coal, and many other raw materials. Other countries have an almost equally rich subsoil, such as Zimbabwe and Zaire with their gold mines. There are precious stones in Kasai, copper ore in Katanga, and oilfields in Nigeria.

Precious woods are harvested just about everywhere, but this African treasure is a two-edged sword. Thousands of acres of forest have been destroyed, resulting in soil erosion and partial sterilization of the continent. Brushfires and the herds of the nomads are completing the destruction of the little vegetation remaining in some regions, adding to the spread of desert areas.

Poorly equipped to harvest and process these resources into manufactured products, Africa has to export its raw materials, the prices of which vary according to market requirements.

Left: Diamond workers
Right: Iron mines in Mauritania

29

WHICH ARE THE GREAT DESERTS OF SOUTHERN AFRICA?

Two impressive deserts extend over parts of southwestern Africa—the Kalahari and the Namib. Nomadic peoples such as the San (Bushmen) live amid beautiful landscapes and a great variety of wild animals.

Tassili-n-Ajjer is not the only open-air museum in Africa. Astonishing rock paintings and drawings also adorn the walls of sites in Tanzania and the Kalahari. These sometimes mysterious works of art conjure up lifestyles and animal life still to be found in these vast, almost desert regions.

The San (Bushmen) are a hunting people who have taken refuge on the edge of the Kalahari, where they lead a very primitive life while clinging to some surprising traditions. They live on roots and berries that the women are skilled at unearthing, and on game that the men hunt with bone arrows dipped in poison extracted from a caterpillar. They are familiar with the stars, as well as the animal life and the plants found in their territory, and they make superb ornaments with bits of ostrich eggshell. They are also talented painters and remarkable dancers.

These people, of whom only a few thousand remain, are unfamiliar with metals, and get along without pottery, fabrics, or adobe houses. Unfortunately for them, however, civilization is gradually forcing them to give up their way of life and become part of modern Africa.

Bushmen (also called San)

30

WHICH IS THE LARGEST ISLAND IN AFRICA?

Madagascar is the largest of the islands (and the fourth largest island in the world). It is especially striking because of its multiracial population, while others, such as Zanzibar and Mauritius, enjoy the reputation of being spice paradises.

From the Red Sea to the Cape of Good Hope, there is a chain of islands some of which were frequented even in ancient times by Egyptian, then Carthaginian, Roman, Chinese, Indian, and finally Arab explorers. On these islands the Arabs established that prosperous trading posts, bridgeheads of their caravan expeditions that went far into the then unknown continent.

Some traces of their temporary presence are found there, and most of their descendants frequent mosques. They have managed to preserve their particular islander traits, while living in harmony with the coast dwellers. Madagascar is the melting pot of a mixture of African and Indonesian populations. The Indonesians brought to it knowledge of their architecture and rice farming. Although rich in ores and precious stones, and formerly an exporter of coffee and spices, Madagascar today is immersed in political problems that have reduced it to a state of great poverty.

Its neighbor, Mauritius, has successfully integrated the various roots making up its population, the majority of which is Indian, and gives a better picture of success. Finally, islands like Réunion and Mayotte have remained French and have the status of "départements"—French administrative districts—or French Overseas Territories. The Seychelles offer tourists landscapes of great beauty.

Top: A mosque in Shela
Bottom left: Dhaw (the Arab port of embarkation in the Indian Ocean)
Bottom right: A Muslim woman in Lamu, Kenya

A

ABYSSINIA : former name of Ethiopia.

AFRICAN NATIONAL CONGRESS : South African political group that is opposed to apartheid; outlawed since 1960, it was finally recognized in 1990 by the government of South Africa as a political party.

AIDS : (A)cquired (I)mmune (D)eficiency (S)yndrome. Sexually transmittable viral disease caused by the HIV virus, which affects the immune system of the body; there is presently no cure.

AKSUM (ALSO SPELLED AXUM) : The Aksum Empire appeared circa 500 B.C. Its power extended to the whole of northern Ethiopia and as far as the Blue Nile in the west and to the depressions in the east. Its prosperity depended on agriculture and trade (myrrh, incense, ivory, gold, slaves, etc.). It was at its height from 520 to 527 A.D., when it dominated southern Arabia, but the spread of Islam in the seventh century led to its becoming isolated. The present city of Aksum was the capital of this flourishing empire that was Christianized as early as the fourth century.

APARTHEID : a policy of segregation and political and economic discrimination practiced in South Africa wherein black citizens and other non-Europeans were denied the right to vote or to travel to certain areas of the country or to live in areas considered "white settlements."

AUSTRALOPITHECA : anthropoid or large tail-less ape, discovered in South Africa. It already knew how to cut stone and produce fire and is considered to be the ancestor of present-day man.

B

BANTU : group of peoples who live in the southern half of the African continent. They include in particular the Shona, the Sotho, the Zulu, the Tswana, the Xhana, the Khoisan, the Tsonga, and the Swazi, and speak interrelated languages.

BLUE NILE (BAHR EL-AZRAK) : river in Ethiopia and Sudan, rising in Lake Tana; it joins the White Nile at Khartum and becomes the Nile.

BOERS : name given to the descendants of the Netherlands colonists who settled in South Africa.

C

CUSH : name given in the time of the pharaohs to the region of the upper Nile valley, between the second and sixth falls of the Nile. A country rich in gold, open to Africa for its ivory and ebony trade, it was soon coveted by the pharaohs, who conquered it in 1530 B.C. From the third century A.D., it began to decline.

D

DJELLABA : loose, woolen, hooded cloak with sleeves and a full skirt; worn by men.

G

GRIS-GRIS : voodoo charm, amulet, or talisman that is believed to bring good luck to some and bad luck to others.

H

HAUSA : people of northern Nigeria and southern Niger. Strongly influenced by Islam, the Hausa are organized as states run by representatives of the noble classes. They practice possession cults wherein individuals in trances are supposed to pass on messages from the gods.

M

MALARIA (OR MARSH FEVER) : a parasitic disease, caused by hematozoa injected into the blood by the bite of a mosquito; the symptoms are bouts of fever.

MANDELA, NELSON (1918–   ): Africa's best known black nationalist leader, a symbol for blacks against the policy of apartheid in South Africa. He joined the African National Congress (ANC) in 1944 and was charged in 1956 with treason. He went into hiding and continued to protest until his arrest in 1962. Imprisoned from 1962 until 1990, he was finally released and became president of the ANC. In August 1990 he called for an end to the armed struggle of the ANC against the South African white government. On May 11, 1994, he became president of South Africa.

MELANIN: a dark brown pigment that gives skin, hair, and iris their color.

MENELIK I: son of the Queen of Sheba and King Solomon of Israel; founder, according to legend, of the dynasty of the emperors of Ethiopia. (Menelik II: emperor of Ethiopia (1889–1913))

MONOTHEISTIC: referring to a religion asserting the existence of only one God.

N

NILOTIC: relating to the Nile, its delta, and riparian countries.

NUBIA: desert-like area of northeastern Africa, extending from Aswan (Egypt) to Khartum (Sudan), and to the neighboring deserts. In the time of the pharaohs, this region was known as the Cush. The Greeks and the Romans called it Ethiopia.

P

PALEONTOLOGIST: an expert specializing in paleontology, that is, the science dealing with beings existing on the earth in prehistoric times, and that is based on the study of fossils.

S

SAHARA (CLIMATE): arid zone, characterized by sparsity and extreme irregularity of precipitation. Spectacular sandstorms are often accompanied by a southeasterly wind (the sirocco) that causes the temperature to rise. The large amount of sunshine sometimes brings record-breaking temperatures—high temperatures of over 50, or even 55 degrees Centigrade (122° to 131°F). Temperature ranges between day and night are varied—15 to 30 degrees Centigrade (59° to 86°F). In winter, low temperatures of less than 0 degrees Centigrade (32°F—freezing point) are sometimes observed.

SCARIFICATION: surface incision on the skin, made with a sharp blade or scarificator.

T

TASSILI: noun of Berber origin meaning plateau. Tassili-n-Ajjer is a mountainous region in the central Sahara, in which prehistoric rock drawings still exist.

TELEKI: Count Samuel Teleki. Born in Hungary, in 1845, to a wealthy noble family, he made an expedition to East Africa from 1886 to 1888. He discovered Lake Rudolph (now Lake Turkana), in northern Kenya and Lake Stefanie in Ethiopia.

W

WHITE NILE (BAHR EL-ABIAD): name given to the Nile in Sudan, between Lake No and its confluent with the Blue Nile.

Y

YORUBA: people of southwest Nigeria, Togo, and Benin. In the fifteenth century they established kingdoms with brilliant civilizations. They are farmers, traders, or craftsmen. They practice animism (the worship of spirits that are part of the natural environment).

B.C.

3000

2589–2566 Reign of Cheops (2589–2566); built the first of the great pyramids at Giza.

First period of the Minoan civilization in Crete. Appearance of metal (2700–2500)

2000

Amenohotep IV introduced worship of the Sun God Aton, and became Ikhnaton. First form of monotheism (1364–1347)

Start of the Mycenian age—Greece (from around 1600)

1000

Nok civilisation—Nigeria (900 B.C. to 200 A.D.)

Founding of Rome (753)

0

After the defeat of Mark Antony and Cleopatra (31), Egypt became a Roman province (30)

First great persecution of Christians (249–251)

500

Capture of Carthage and conquest of Morocco by the Arabs (700)

Beginning of the Moorish domination of Spain (711)

1000

The Arab writer Ibn Battuta's voyage of discovery through the western Sahara to Senegal and Tombouctou (Timbuktu) (1352)

Richard I, Lionheart, king of England (1189–1199)

1500

Portuguese explored Africa's west coast.

Start of the slave trade to the Americas.

1600

Founding of Cape Town and of the colony of the same name by the Dutch East India Company (1652)

The Pilgrims landed in America (1620)

1700

Conquest of Zanzibar by Omani Arabs (1730): The island becomes a base for the slave trade in eastern Africa.

End of the French and Indian War (1763)

1800

The British occupy Cape Colony (1806) Boer War (1899–1902)

Civil War (1861–1865)

1900

Founding of the Union of South Africa (1910) dominant power of the white minority

U.S. enters World War I (1917)

A.D.

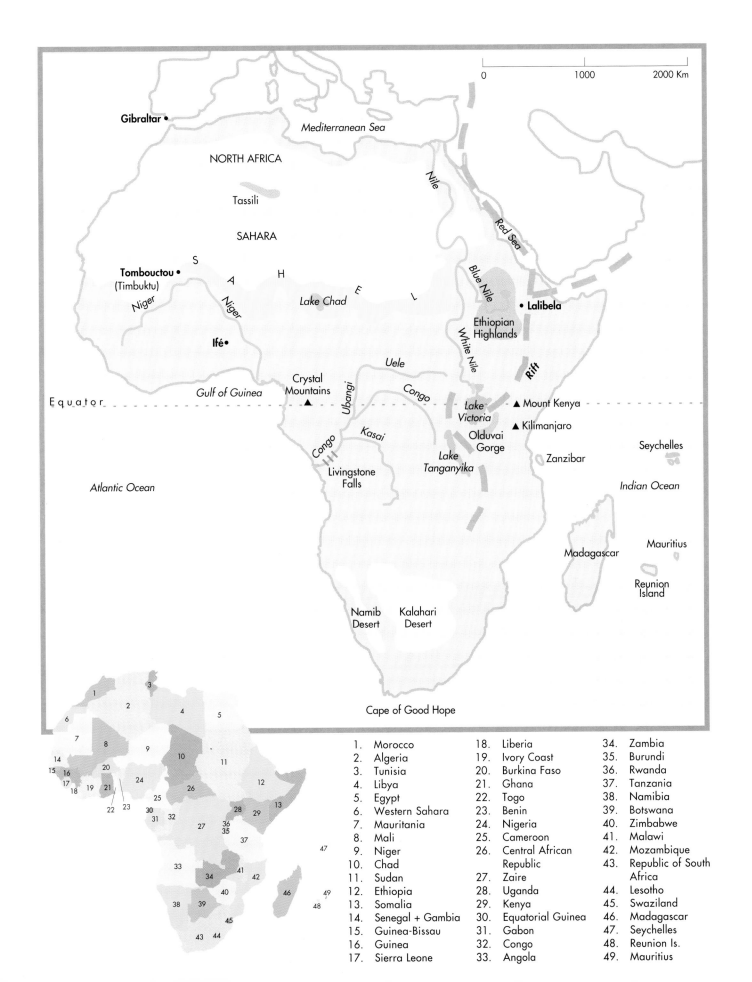

Gibraltar •

Mediterranean Sea

NORTH AFRICA

Tassili

SAHARA

S

Tombouctou •
(Timbuktu)

A   H

E

Niger   Niger   Lake Chad   L

Ifé •

Nile

Red Sea

Blue Nile

White Nile

• **Lalibela**

Ethiopian
Highlands

Rift

Crystal
Mountains ▲

Uele

Ubangi   Congo

Gulf of Guinea

Equator

Congo   Kasai

Livingstone
Falls

Lake
Victoria

Olduvai
Gorge

▲ Mount Kenya

▲ Kilimanjaro

Lake
Tanganyika

Zanzibar

Seychelles

Atlantic Ocean

Indian Ocean

Madagascar

Mauritius

Reunion
Island

Namib
Desert

Kalahari
Desert

Cape of Good Hope

1. Morocco	18. Liberia	34. Zambia
2. Algeria	19. Ivory Coast	35. Burundi
3. Tunisia	20. Burkina Faso	36. Rwanda
4. Libya	21. Ghana	37. Tanzania
5. Egypt	22. Togo	38. Namibia
6. Western Sahara	23. Benin	39. Botswana
7. Mauritania	24. Nigeria	40. Zimbabwe
8. Mali	25. Cameroon	41. Malawi
9. Niger	26. Central African	42. Mozambique
10. Chad	Republic	43. Republic of South
11. Sudan	27. Zaire	Africa
12. Ethiopia	28. Uganda	44. Lesotho
13. Somalia	29. Kenya	45. Swaziland
14. Senegal + Gambia	30. Equatorial Guinea	46. Madagascar
15. Guinea-Bissau	31. Gabon	47. Seychelles
16. Guinea	32. Congo	48. Reunion Is.
17. Sierra Leone	33. Angola	49. Mauritius

index

bibliography

AFRICA, FOR READERS FROM 7 TO 77 YEARS

Bailey, Bernadine.
Madagascar in Pictures.
Minneapolis: Lerner Publications, 1988.

Baschet, Eric.
Africa 1900.
Switzerland: Swan Productions, 1989.

Bennett, Norman Robert.
Africa and Europe from Roman Times to the Present.
New York: Africana Pub. Co., 1975.

Bohannan, Paul.
Africa and Africans.
Prospect Heights, Ill.: Waveland Press, 1988.

Capstick, Peter Hathaway.
The Last Ivory Hunter: The Saga of Wally Johnson.
New York: St. Martin's Press, 1988.

Cheney, Patricia.
The Land and People of Zimbabwe.
1st ed. New York: Lippincott, 1990.

Clinton, Susan.
Henry Stanley and David Livingstone.
Chicago: Children's Press, 1990.

Cloudsley-Thompson, J. L., ed.
Sahara Desert.
New York: Pergamon Press, 1984.

Denenberg, Barry.
*Nelson Mandela: "No Easy Walk to Freedom":
A Biography.*
New York: Scholastic, 1991.

Fitzgerald, Mary Anne.
Nomad.
New York: Viking, 1993.

Forbath, Peter.
The River Congo: The Discovery.
New York: Harper & Row, 1977.

Houston, Dick.
Safari Adventure.
New York: Dutton, 1991.

Leslie-Melville, Betty.
*Elephants Have Right of Way: Life with the Wild
Animals of Africa.*
New York: Doubleday Books for Young Readers, 1992.

Lester, Julius.
*How Many Spots Does a Leopard Have? And Other
Tales.*
New York: Scholastic, 1989.

Mazrui, Ali Alamin.
The Africans: A Triple Heritage.
Boston: Little, Brown, 1986.

Naylor, Kim.
*Discovery Guide to West Africa: The Niger and
Gambia River Route.*
Hippocrene, 1989.

Ngubane, Harriet.
Zulus of Southern Africa.
Vero Beach, Fl.: Rourke Publications, 1987.

Nugent, Rory.
*Drums Along the Congo: On the Trail of the Last Living
Dinosaur.*
Boston: Houghton Mifflin, 1993.

Paton, Jonathan.
The Land and People of South Africa.
1st ed. New York: Lippincott, 1990.

Rissik, Dee.
South Africa.
New York: M. Cavendish, 1992.

Rossellini, Albert.
Côte d'Ivoire (Ivory Coast) in Pictures.
Minneapolis: Lerner Publications Co., 1988.

Smith, Anthony.
Great Rift.
New York: Sterling, 1988.

Taylor, Dave.
Endangered Savannah Animals.
Niagara-on-the-Lake, Ont.: Crabtree Pub., 1993.

Taylor, Jane.
Fielding's African Safaris.
New York: Fielding Travel Books, 1987.

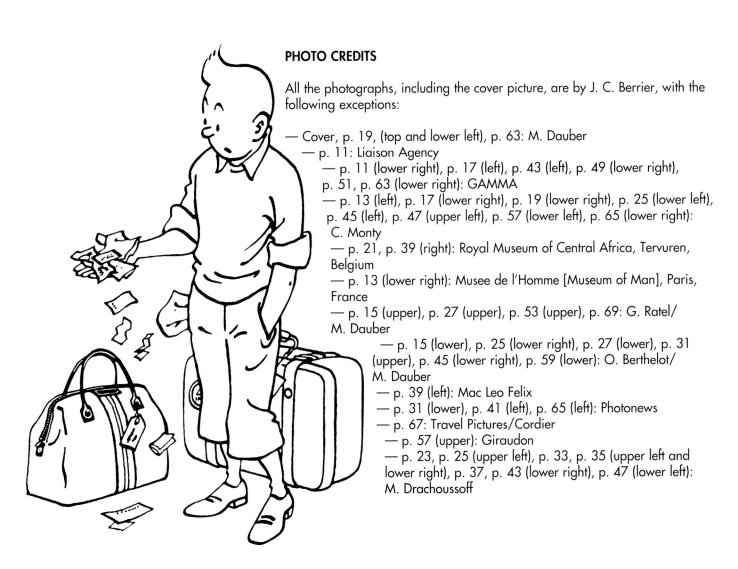

PHOTO CREDITS

All the photographs, including the cover picture, are by J. C. Berrier, with the following exceptions:

— Cover, p. 19, (top and lower left), p. 63: M. Dauber
— p. 11: Liaison Agency
— p. 11 (lower right), p. 17 (left), p. 43 (left), p. 49 (lower right), p. 51, p. 63 (lower right): GAMMA
— p. 13 (left), p. 17 (lower right), p. 19 (lower right), p. 25 (lower left), p. 45 (left), p. 47 (upper left), p. 57 (lower left), p. 65 (lower right): C. Monty
— p. 21, p. 39 (right): Royal Museum of Central Africa, Tervuren, Belgium
— p. 13 (lower right): Musee de l'Homme [Museum of Man], Paris, France
— p. 15 (upper), p. 27 (upper), p. 53 (upper), p. 69: G. Ratel/ M. Dauber
— p. 15 (lower), p. 25 (lower right), p. 27 (lower), p. 31 (upper), p. 45 (lower right), p. 59 (lower): O. Berthelot/ M. Dauber
— p. 39 (left): Mac Leo Felix
— p. 31 (lower), p. 41 (left), p. 65 (left): Photonews
— p. 67: Travel Pictures/Cordier
— p. 57 (upper): Giraudon
— p. 23, p. 25 (upper left), p. 33, p. 35 (upper left and lower right), p. 37, p. 43 (lower right), p. 47 (lower left): M. Drachoussoff

Titles in the *Tintin's Travel Diaries* series: